i WANT TO
BE ON
TV

RED FOX READ ALONE

It takes a special book to be a
RED FOX READ ALONE!

If you enjoy this book, why not
choose another READ ALONE
from the list?

I WANT TO BE ON TV

Penny Speller

illustrated by Susanna Kendall

RED FOX

A Red Fox Book

Published by The Random House Group Ltd
20 Vauxhall Bridge Road, London, SW1V 2SA

A division of The Random House Group Ltd
London Melbourne Sydney Auckland
Johannesburg and agencies throughout the world

3 5 7 9 10 8 6 4 2

First published by Andersen Press Limited 1991
Red Fox edition 1992

This Red Fox edition 1999

Printed and bound in Great Britain by
Cox & Wyman Limited, Reading, Berkshire

Papers used by Random House UK Limited are natural, recyclable products
made from wood grown in sustainable forests. The manufacturing processes
conform to the environmental regulations of the country of origin.

RANDOM HOUSE UK Limited Reg. No. 954009

www.randomhouse.co.uk

ISBN 0 09 940183 5

Troy Benson had an ambition. It was no secret.

'I'm going to be on telly when I grow up,' he declared, 'or even before.'

That was why he had so much to talk to his friend Mark about on the way home from school.

5

'It's fantastic,' he said as he grabbed Mark's arm at the school gate. The jerk almost brought Mark down on top of him.

'You don't have to pull my arm off just because there's a TV company coming to film at the school,' said Mark.

'But this could be my lucky break,' said Troy.

'You heard Mrs Stanley, didn't you?' said Mark. 'The film people are coming to make a film about teaching and we are to keep out of the way.'

'She said they'd be filming some classes though, didn't she?' said Troy.

'Only classes doing boring old work,' Mark reminded him. 'I can't imagine why they want to film that.'

'I'm going to make sure they film me,' said Troy.

'How?' asked Mark. They had reached Mark's front gate and this question brought them to a stop. Troy shrugged his shoulders. He imagined cameras in front of him.

'I'll find a way,' he said, looking into them. 'You'll see.'

He started to scrape his shoe along the edge of the pavement. Mark was right, it wasn't going to be easy. There were so many children in the school and the programme was supposed to be about teachers. He could see that the chances of being filmed were small.

'I've got to do it,' he said. His lips tightened as he thought.

'Troy, you look like you've got belly-ache,' said Mark.

Troy screwed up his face even more and clutched his stomach.

'Good-bye,' he groaned and staggered onto the steps to his flat. He wasn't looking where he was going and bumped into his older brother Leon.

'Look out, Troy!' said Leon. 'You walked straight into me.'

'Sorry,' muttered Troy. He looked down at the grey concrete.

'Hey, man, what's up?' said Leon.

'It's tomorrow,' said Troy. 'There's a TV crew coming to school and we might be filmed.'

'Sounds like good news to me,' said Leon. 'It's what you've always wanted and it'll mean less work.'

'But I need to make sure I'm on the film,' said Troy. 'Even if it means I have to be working to do it.'

'Listen, man,' said Leon. 'If you want to get noticed, you gotta dress

for the part. It's how you look that
counts.'

He sat on the step and patted
Troy.

'Yeah, you're right,' said Troy.
'Thanks for the help.' He darted up
the last few steps to the front door.

'No trouble,' said Leon and he
carried on down.

Mrs Benson was hoovering the sitting
room when Troy came in.

'You've been scraping those shoes
again,' she said. 'If you wear out
another pair in only a month, I swear
I'll make you go barefoot to school.
How about some tea?'

'I need to sort out my clothes,
Mum,' said Troy. He ran straight off

to his bedroom without stopping to put his bag down.

'Well, I know miracles happen but I never thought I'd actually live to see one,' she called after him.

There were two things which Troy felt were perfect to wear, two of his best possessions. One was a pair of black patent leather lace-up shoes. He had had a battle to get them; they were expensive, but Troy had reminded his mother how smart he would look on Sundays when he went to church and she gave in. Then there were the red and yellow check Bermuda shorts. Troy fished them out of the drawer and laid them on the bed. They had been a birthday present from his uncle who lived in America and Troy reckoned they were the only pair like it anywhere.

'But what else?' he asked himself.
Troy carefully went through his
drawers until the outfit was complete.

There was his red Michael Jackson
T-shirt, the shorts, his sister's yellow
socks, the shoes and Leon's black and
red check cap. Troy stood back and
felt very pleased with his selection
until he remembered he was going to
have to get this lot past his mum.

'She'll never let me,' he thought.
He saw the cameras in front of him
again. 'I'll just have to hide them in
my bag and change on the way to
school. It's the only way, even if I'm
late.'

The headmaster, Mr Buchan, had said they were to treat it like an ordinary day, but how could it be when Troy's dream was so near to coming true? Not everyone in the class could tell you what 7 times 4 was just like that, but they all knew that Troy Benson wanted to be on telly. Sometimes he got teased for it.

'You've got to be clever to get a job on telly,' Tom Banks had boasted to him. 'And you've got to be tall. My dad told me.'

Troy didn't find school work easy. Sometimes he found it very hard to keep up. He thought Tom was probably right. Most of the people you see on telly look clever; they look like the sort of people who do well at school, especially the newsreaders. Troy would have liked to be a newsreader or a reporter. He was small too. Even his best friend Mark was taller. It all went through Troy's mind as he hurried to school in the morning. It was a windy day and he had to hold his hand over his hat to stop it blowing off. He had hidden in the bin cupboards to change his clothes and was late, but today would be different. He felt as if a beautifully

wrapped present had fallen out of the
sky and landed at his feet. The TV
cameras would be in his school and
Troy knew this had to be meant for
him.

He caught a glimpse of his
reflection in the classroom window
and imagined himself looking into the
camera. His thick black hair was
curling out under the hat. He smiled
and his eyes became rounder and
bright.

It was all going so well that Troy
walked into the classroom feeling good
all over and was very surprised when
Mrs Stanley just stared at him

without speaking. It seemed a long
time before she said,

'Troy Benson, do you really think
that outfit is suitable for school?'

'It was all I had clean, Miss,' said
Troy.

'Well I haven't got time to discuss
it now,' she said. 'Everyone is to go
to the hall this morning for an
announcement and I want you all to
line up. For goodness' sake, you can
at least take that hat off.'

Troy reluctantly pulled off his hat and lined up with the others. Outside the classroom he could see a big van parked. He wanted to skip with excitement as they walked down the corridor into the hall.

'You'll be in trouble when Mr Buchan sees you,' whispered Mark.

'At least I'll get noticed,' said Troy. 'I'm the one they'll be looking at.'

In the hall, the first thing Troy noticed was the number of people gathered around Mr Buchan.

'It must be a very important film if so many people are needed to make it,' he whispered to Mark.

'Not if it's about teachers,' Mark whispered back.

One person caught his attention straight away. She was very tall, with dark curly hair down to her shoulders and large red earrings in the shape of hoops. She wore a red jacket and a green skirt full of gathers. Troy knew she must be someone important. He looked down at his own bright clothes and smiled to himself. She was going to be impressed when she saw him.

Mr Buchan stood up and held a piece of paper out in front of him.

'I would like to introduce you to the team of people who will be filming in the school. They each have a job to do here today and if you see any of these people around the school you will know who they are and, I trust, will not get in their way.

'I have here the arrangements for the day's filming. I have consulted the

Director, Mrs Liptrott, who is standing here beside me, and we have decided that filming in the morning will include Classes 1 and 2 in their classrooms and Classes 5 and 6 in the hall for music. This afternoon Classes 9 and 10 will be filmed outside playing games.

'I would like to remind you that this filming is for an item about teachers and it is the staff who are mainly involved. I hope that I can rely on you all to behave as the sensible people that you are and my advice is that you try to pretend that the cameras are not here.'

Troy's heart sank. A cruel blow had been dealt and for a moment he was blind to everything that went on around him. His class had not been chosen. He was not going to be filmed.

Tom Banks jogged his arm and he realised that everyone was leaving the hall. He followed the line out, thinking only about his disappointment. He didn't even

remember that no one had noticed his clothes.

'You'll have to think of something pretty amazing if you're going to get in on the act now,' said Mark when they were back at the classroom.

'I will,' said Troy, but he had no idea what.

They were supposed to be starting a new workbook but Mrs Stanley was looking flustered.

'This film business has quite disorganised me,' she said. 'I've forgotten to get that new set of books. I'll need a volunteer to go and collect them for me from the hall.'

Troy knew that the book cupboard was off the hall and the hall was where this morning's filming was to take place. His hand went up like a shot and he pushed himself up off his chair to make himself look taller.

'Yes all right, Troy,' said Mrs Stanley. 'I can see you well enough in those clothes without you having to stand up. Go to the hall and ask Mr Buchan if you can have the pile of workbooks.' Troy leaped up from the chair trying to hide the enormous smile which was forcing its way onto his face. This produced a strange expression and Mrs Stanley looked worried.

'Troy, are you in pain?' she asked.

'No, Miss, I feel fine,' he said. He was so worried that she might ask him to sit down again that the smile vanished.

His heart pounded as he raced along the corridor. He could see a

group of people in the hall doorway
and wires all over the floor. A man
pushed past with a huge light. Troy
stood for a moment watching. Each
person seemed to be doing something,

but Troy couldn't tell what it all had to do with filming. He recognised Mrs Liptrott in the middle of the hall shouting numbers to someone at the other end. He imagined himself as a reporter. He pretended to be standing with a microphone, ready to walk across the hall floor, when a voice behind him said:

'I thought I noticed some very bright colours in the hall this morning.'

25

Troy was so surprised that he nearly let out a yell.

'Mr Buchan,' he said. He was angry at having been pulled away from the world of filming.

'You're not supposed to be wandering around the school like a lost boy with no home to go to. I trust that you are now going to provide me with one of those excuses that you are so famous for,' said Mr Buchan.

Troy didn't like this way of talking. He couldn't always tell whether Mr Buchan was being funny or not and he'd rather just be told off.

'Mrs Stanley sent me,' he said. 'She asked me to

collect some books from the cupboard.'

'In view of the current upheaval, I shall fetch the books myself. You may wait here by the door and keep out of the way.'

It was useless. There was no way anyone was going to notice him amongst all this activity, even dressed as he was. Mr Buchan brought over the pile of books and Troy carried them back to class.

Troy thought hard, but he only had one idea that morning.

'Don't be silly,' whispered Mark. 'It'll never work in a million years.'

'I'll try it anyway,' said Troy. He put up his hand.

'What is it, Troy?' asked Mrs Stanley.

'I think I saw a rabbit in the corridor, Miss,' said Troy.

'A what!' exclaimed Mrs Stanley.

'A rabbit, Miss,' said Troy. 'They've got a rabbit in Class 2 and I think I saw it in the corridor. It must have escaped. I'll go and catch it if you like and take it back.'

Mrs Stanley raised her eyebrows
and instead of sending him straight
off, she gave Troy a stare. He
guessed that she wasn't going to
believe him. She walked over to the
door, opened it, looked up and down
the corridor and came back.

'Troy, I think you could do a lot
worse than to confine your
imagination to your story writing,' she
said.

'Does that mean you don't want me to go and look for it?' asked Troy.

'Yes,' said Mrs Stanley.

'Why can't teachers just tell you off?' Troy whispered to Mark. 'Then you'd know what they mean.'

At morning playtime, Troy and Mark sat on the tarmac by the railings and tried to come up with their most brilliant plan ever. Troy pretended to be holding a camera and filming the rest of the playground. Neither of them had been able to think of anything when a voice called out, 'Mark dear, is that you?'

They turned round to see Mark's mother on the other side of the railings with a bag of shopping in one hand and a lunchbox in the other. Troy compared Mark to his mother in

29

the camera. Mark was skinny, but his mother was as round as she was tall and always out of breath.

'I am glad,' she said. 'Robert forgot his lunch this morning and I was going to take it in but I can give it to you now, can't I? You can run over to Class 2 and save me the bother. See you later, love.'

She passed the lunchbox through the railings.

'Thank you, madam,' said Troy He pretended to switch off his camera. 'Tomorrow you will be a star.'

'What are you playing at, Troy?' she asked. 'Does your mother know you're wearing those shoes?'

'Er... 'bye, Mum,' said Mark and he pulled Troy away.

Robert was Mark's younger brother and he always brought sandwiches to school.

'Listen, Mark,' said Troy, 'I'll take the lunchbox for you and you can have a rest. You look tired.'

'Go on. Say it,' said Mark. 'They're supposed to be filming Class 2 and you want to go in case you get on telly.'

'It would make a good scene, wouldn't it?' said Troy. 'Showing how helpful they've taught us to be. Anyway, you have to let me go; I'm your best friend.'

'That's true,' said Mark. 'Okay, but make sure you don't forget to give Robert his lunchbox when you've suddenly become famous. I'll be in trouble if you do.' That was what Troy liked so much about Mark. He was the kind of boy who would always help out a friend.

Just then the bell rang and they had to line up for class. As soon as Mrs Stanley appeared, Troy held up the lunchbox.

'Please, Miss,' he said. 'Robert Lawson forgot his lunchbox and Mrs Lawson asked me to take it.'

Mrs Stanley frowned.

'Why did she ask you and not Mark?' she asked. Mark turned his head to avoid looking at her.

'I was just playing by the gate and she asked me,' said Troy. 'I guess she didn't see Mark.'

'Oh very well,' said Mrs Stanley. 'But Robert doesn't need it now so you can take it later. I want you all to watch a programme.'

It was agony for Troy. The class had been doing a project on garden wildlife and Mrs Stanley had promised to show them a programme about worms and snails and things. Troy couldn't concentrate. It would soon be lunchtime and he would have to take the lunchbox. Cameras were running only a few metres away and he felt like a prisoner waiting for his freedom. His body did not want to sit still and his mind couldn't think about snails. At last it was finished.

'Troy,' said Mrs Stanley. 'You had better run along with that lunchbox. The rest of you can tidy up and go back to your seats.'

Troy stood up with the lunchbox. He had not let go of it once. This could be his ticket to stardom.

Once again he was running down the corridor with his heart pounding. His legs felt like jelly.

'This could be stage-fright,' he said
to himself. 'Actors get it.'

He could feel his forehead getting
wet from sweat. He wiped his arm
across his face and stopped. The door

of Class 2 opened and out came Mrs
Liptrott and Mr Buchan. They
walked away in the other direction.
They were talking and they didn't
notice him.

Troy walked up to the door and looked in. The cameras were there all right, and the lights and instruments with wires, but they had stopped. It was finished. They were packing up.

Troy thought he was going to be sick. Mrs Jackson, the teacher, came to the door.

'What is it, Troy?' she asked.

'Robert's lunchbox,' he said, but the words came out croaky.

'Thank you,' said Mrs Jackson. Troy turned to walk away. 'Are you all right, Troy?' she called out.

'Yes,' muttered Troy, but he dared not turn round. He was crying. No matter how hard he tried to force back the tears, he was crying. Where could he go now? Not back to the classroom looking like this. He went into the toilets where he stood and bit his lip and held his breath till he nearly choked. He forced his eyes to open wide and gradually the tears stopped. He hung his head over the sink and splashed water on his face. He lifted his shirt to dry it. What did

a stupid shirt matter now? He darted back to the classroom. If Mrs Stanley had seen that Troy had been crying, she said nothing. Troy was relieved but he could still feel the anger and the tears waiting to escape.

After lunch, Troy went outside with Mark and they talked.

'What happened?' his friend wanted to know.

'Nothing,' said Troy. 'Nothing! Nothing! Nothing! Nothing!'

'I knew it was a no hoper,' said Mark. 'We just don't have a plan that will work.'

'It's no good,' said Troy. 'And look at my shirt.' Troy's shirt was beginning to look grubby. It was now stained with gravy as well as sweat.

'Don't worry about the shirt,' said Mark. 'Stains don't show up on telly. What you need is to do something special or really exciting. Then they'll

want to interview you and not silly old Class 9.'

Troy said nothing. His head was blank. Mark was getting more excited and couldn't see his despair.

Delphine and Rachel came over.

'Tom Banks says he saw you crying in the toilets,' said Delphine. 'He says you're trying to get into the film and that's why you're wearing those silly clothes and keep showing off.'

'Go away,' said Mark.

'Is it true?' asked Delphine.

'Of course it is,' snapped Troy.

'How will you do it?' asked Delphine.

'I'm not telling,' said Troy.

'That's 'cause you don't know. You can't do it,' said Delphine.

'I can and I will and you can tell Tom Banks from me that he doesn't know anything,' shouted Troy. He could see Tom standing on the far side of the playground. He was watching Troy. Troy deliberately turned his head away and walked off. Mark ran after him.

'Break your leg,' said Troy.

'I thought you liked me,' said Mark.

''Course I do. I just want you to pretend to break your leg so that I can rescue you,' said Troy.

'It's an idea,' said Mark, but then he thought about it and added, 'Do you think it'll work?'

'No,' said Troy. 'You're not a very good actor.'

'I don't know what a broken leg looks like. I don't know if I could pretend the right things. They might even take me to hospital.'

The bell went for afternoon school.

During the afternoon, Troy began to feel quite desperate. School would soon be over. The classroom looked out over the playground and he could see the film crew setting up their equipment.

42

Troy whispered to Mark, 'I've got another idea.'
His hand went up.
'Yes?' asked Mrs Stanley.

'I think I heard the fire alarm, Miss,' he said. The rest of the class laughed.

I didn't,' said Mrs Stanley. 'But
m sure that if you did we shall all
hear it soon. Meanwhile, why don't
you get on with your work.'

Tom Banks sneered at Troy. Troy
looked out of the window. Grey
clouds were gathering in the sky. It
seemed to get dull suddenly and the
air felt colder.

'I hope it rains all over them,' Troy
thought to himself. 'I hope it ruins
their cameras and their film.'

Mrs Stanley had noticed the clouds
too.

'It looks as if it might rain,' she
said. 'I want you all to go outside and
look for worms this afternoon so
perhaps you had better do it now. We

need them for this tank.' She pointed to a square glass container. 'We'll also need plenty of soil for them so perhaps some of you can collect that instead. If you all take a jar from beside the sink and one of the old spoons, you can all go outside and see

how many worms you can find. One small reminder; don't destroy the plants in the flower-bed over there or we'll all be in trouble.'

'Come on,' said Mark. 'You can watch the filming out there.'

'You could try breaking a leg this time,' said Troy. 'It's the best chance we'll get.' He grabbed a jar and a spoon.

'Supposing I end up with my leg in plaster?' said Mark.

'It would be a small sacrifice,' said Troy.

Tom Banks brushed past them.

'Are those your best worm collecting shoes?' he laughed. Tom was very tall for his age and had dark hair and eyes. No one liked to argue with him. Troy felt his neck tighten but he walked away. Outside he could see the cameras set up to film Class 9 on the patch of grass which was always known as 'the field'. It wasn't a real field, not even the size of a

football pitch, but it was flat and grassy and the children played sports there in the summer. Around the edge of the concrete playground were circles of flower-beds. Nothing grew very well because the children were always trampling on them, but Mr Duffy the caretaker never gave up trying. Most of the others made a dash for these but Troy decided he would look for worms on the field. Mark went with him. They stooped down at the edge of the grass, poking their spoons about. Mark lifted up a lump of earth and revealed a fat pink

worm squirming in the open air. For
a moment, Troy forgot himself. He
picked up the worm with two fingers
and held it out. He could see
Delphine nearby with her back to
him.

'The giant worm's coming to get you. Run for it,' he yelled as he ran towards her with the worm wriggling in his fingers. Delphine jumped up and screamed.

'That's enough of that, Troy,' Mrs Stanley called over.

Troy took the worm back to Mark and left it on the grass.

'I'm going over there,' said Troy, pointing to the far side of the field. To get there he would have to walk right behind Mrs Liptrott and the cameraman. Mr Buchan was there too.

'Don't,' said Mark. 'You'll be in for it.'

'I can't just sit here and dig up worms,' said Troy. 'That's not how you get noticed.'

'You'll only get into trouble in front of everyone,' said Mark. 'You don't have an excuse.'

'We are supposed to be looking for worms, aren't we?' said Troy. 'It'll all be over before we come up with another plan.'

He stood up feeling shaky. He began to walk slowly across the field. He could see the creases in the back of Mrs Liptrott's jacket. He could smell the perfume of the lady with the clipboard. He could see the mud on their polished shoes.

'Troy Benson!' A shout stopped him at once. He turned round. Mrs

50

Stanley was waving to him and
Delphine stood beside her pointing.

'Troy, come back here,' she
shouted.

The lady with the clipboard turned
round and smiled at Troy. He
couldn't move. He didn't want to go.

Mark ran up and grabbed his arm and pulled him back towards the classroom.

'I was nearly there,' Troy shouted. 'You stupid idiot. I was about to make it.'

'You were about to get into trouble,' said Mark. 'You don't think

they want a film about teachers shouting, do you?'

They walked back to the classroom, not talking. The grey clouds had thickened and the light was growing darker.

'We could be in for a thunderstorm,' said Mrs Stanley as they all filed back into the classroom.

Troy and Mark didn't look at each other and sat down on separate sides of the room. Mrs Stanley filled the

tank with earth and put in the worms. Various children helped but Troy had no interest and Mark looked away from him. Troy could see that

his friend was right, but it had all
seemed so near and so possible. Now
he could see them packing up
outside. The filming was over and
he'd rowed with Mark.

School finished. Delphine smiled at
Troy on her way out.
  'I guess you'll just have to be
famous another day,' she said.

  Troy picked up his hat and walked
out. He could feel a great hole of
nothing inside him. No film. No
friend.

Mark was waiting at the gate for Robert. Troy had to walk right past him. They looked at each other and Troy saw the freckles on his friend's face flicker as a smile broke out. Troy smiled too.

'I'm sorry about the film,' said Mark. 'I know you'll be on telly one day.'

'You'd better believe it,' said Troy. He could feel tears gathering in his eyes again. Spots of rain began to fall onto his face.

'C'mon.' said Mark. 'Let's get home. Maybe you can come for tea.'

'Not yet,' said Troy. 'I just want to watch them go.'

'I'm not staying,' said Mark. 'I've got Robert and it's about to tip down. See you tomorrow.' He ran off with Robert following.

Gradually the school cleared and the road outside became empty again. By now it was beginning to rain quite heavily. Troy was glad of a chance to disguise his tears. He sat on the wall, feeling his body get wetter and wetter and watching the camera crew rushing about. He pretended he had a camera again, filming the film crew. He could see that there were two cameramen and two people to hold microphones, someone who had sat by a box of dials all day and a woman who was clearly meant to look after the lights. He moved the camera along. A man was standing looking at him. It was the reporter, the one who had spoken in front of the camera. Troy dropped his hands.

'Fancy yourself as a cameraman?'

asked the reporter. Troy then noticed
that the man was quite small.

'I'd rather have your job,' said
Troy. 'I'm gonna be on telly one
day.'

'You'll have to work hard,' said the
reporter. 'Lots of people want to be
on telly.'

'So how did you do it?' asked
Troy. The reporter pulled his coat up

round his neck and came over to Troy.

'Truth is,' he said, 'I always liked poking my nose into other people's business. I was better at that than schoolwork. Of course working hard at school and passing some of my exams helped. You'll need to do that too.' He nudged Troy and smiled at him. 'This is going out on the late news tonight. Perhaps your folks will let you stay up and watch it. 'Bye now and good luck.'

He dashed over to his car, jumped in and was gone.

Troy ran home. He was wet through to his skin, but he didn't care. He was thinking about the reporter's advice. His mother was horrified.

'Troy! What d'you think you're playing at, wearing your best clothes to school? Look at you – filthy, soaked.'

'Sorry.' He smiled at her.

'Come in and get dry.' She smiled back.

'I'm gonna be a reporter when I grow up,' said Troy while his mum rubbed his hair with a towel. 'On the telly.'

'Reporter now, is it?' she laughed. 'Thought you were going to do a game show.'

'Changed my mind,' said Troy. 'I've got to stay up and watch the late news tonight. Our school's on. Not me though.'

Troy was tired and lay curled up on the sofa in his pyjamas waiting for the school report. Most of the news was boring; he couldn't understand it. Then the scene changed in a flash and it was his own school hall. It made him smile to see such a familiar place on the television. There was Mr Buchan, there was the reporter talking to him, there was Class 5 all sitting in a circle behind them. Then the scene changed and it was outside on the field. Mr Buchan again and Class 9 running about. Troy's eyes grew heavy and he yawned. His head dropped.

'Hey, man, there's Troy,' said Leon.

Troy's eyes were open and he stared. For a few seconds the television screen held a picture of Troy racing around in the playground with the worm in his hand. He was

pulling a funny face and waving his arms about. The camera had been turned on him and he hadn't even noticed. Now here he was being a fool in front of thousands of people.

'I don't believe it,' said Troy.

'Didn't know they had lessons in madness at your school,' said Leon. 'You must be top of the class.'

Then the film stopped. There was a large picture of Troy, smiling out at everyone while the voice continued to say things about money and tests.

'You look real smart,' said his mum smiling. 'My boy on telly, who'd 'ave thought.'

Troy suddenly felt very happy.

'That was nothing,' he said, yawning. 'Next time I'll be talking as well.'